TO: Benjamin
A magical story
for a magical you

From:

Oh no!
The wizards were in BIG trouble!

A wicked witch had cast
an evil spell completely covering
their magical kingdom in
slimy and extremely smelly goo!
ALL of the wizards were trapped!

4

The wizards really needed someone to help them catch the wicked witch, but who?

The wise old grand wizard looked through his special telescope, and spotted someone who might just be able to help them.

"Quickly! Send Magical Master Owl to ask for Benjamin's help in saving us from the wicked witch!" shouted the wizard.

Magical Master Owl knew he had to help so he flapped and fluttered as swiftly as he could to find the boy spotted through the telescope.

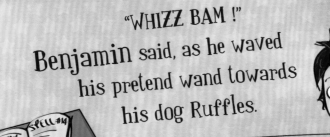

"WHIZZ BAM !"

Benjamin said, as he waved his pretend wand towards his dog Ruffles.

"Oh Ruffles you are supposed to turn into a flying dog."

Benjamin SO wanted to be a Wizard.

8

Suddenly with a flitter and a flap, Magical Master Owl squawked through Benjamin's window into the bedroom and explained (in his best owlish) the trouble the wizards were in, and asked a shocked Benjamin if he could help.

"Of course!"
said a delighted Benjamin.

So Magical Master Owl squawked three times, flapped his wings four times, and with a WHIZZ PUFF, a broomstick, cape and magic wand suddenly appeared!

Benjamin put on the cape,
picked up the wand,
and jumped on his brand
new broomstick.

Quick as a flash
they zoomed out of
Benjamin's window to look
for the wicked witch.

11

The wicked witch was flying around, covering everything and everyone with her yucky, smelly green goo.

"Wahahaha!" she cackled, "Soon the whole world will be covered in my smelly goo and there are no wizards here to stop me!"

12

But little did she realize that **Benjamin** was on his way.

He zoomed under bridges...

...and over houses, looking for the goo-spreading witch.

13

Suddenly Ruffles made
a big booming **bark**.
His super-smelling nose had caught
a whiff of the wicked witch, but she
was too far away for **Benjamin**
to cast a spell on her.

Benjamin clicked
his heels, gripped his
broomstick even tighter,
and zoomed at supersonic speed
towards the wicked witch.

15

Finally Benjamin caught up with the wicked witch.

"Who are you?" the wicked witch sneered, as she launched a massive dollop of sticky green goo at Benjamin.

With lightning speed
Benjamin waved his magic wand.
"BIZZ POP GOO I will stop you!" he shouted.
A huge brightly-colored umbrella appeared,
deflecting all of the smelly goo.

17

The wicked witch squealed with anger, zapping another dollop of smelly green goo towards Benjamin.

"WHIZZ SPLAT send me your hat!" Benjamin shouted.

The witch's hat flew off her head, catching all of her smelly green goo. Yuck!

The witch couldn't believe what this boy wizard was doing!

18

"ZIP ZAP, you will be
trapped in your hat!"
Benjamin cast another spell.

The witch's goo-filled hat
flew back to her,
squashing down
over her head,
squishing
her in the
smelly
green goo.

Hurray the wicked witch was trapped!

19

A triumphant
Benjamin took the
wicked witch back to
the wizards' castle.

All the slippery, slimy green
goo had now gone thanks to
Benjamin breaking the bad witch's
horrible spell.

The wizards were so grateful to
Benjamin that they let him keep the cape,
broomstick AND magic wand!

Benjamin finally felt like a true wizard!

The End